WITHDRAWN
No longer the property of the
Boston Public Library.
Sale of this material benefits the Library.

P9-CEA-819

For Jon Hirsch, the cat's meow
—L. N.

For my beautiful Romeo
—E. O.

SIMON & SCHUSTER BOOKS FOR YOUNG READERS
An imprint of Simon & Schuster Children's Publishing Division
1230 Avenue of the Americas, New York, New York 10020
Text copyright © 2001 by Lesléa Newman
Illustrations copyright © 2001 by Erika Oller

All rights reserved including the right of reproduction in whole or in part in any form.
SIMON & SCHUSTER BOOKS FOR YOUNG READERS is a trademark of Simon & Schuster.

Book design by Jennifer Reyes
The text of this book is set in 16-point Weiss.
The illustrations are rendered in watercolor.
Printed in Hong Kong
2 4 6 8 10 9 7 5 3
Library of Congress Cataloging-in-Publication Data
Newman, Lesléa.
Cats, cats, cats! / Lesléa Newman ; illustrations by Erika Oller.
p. cm.
Summary: At night when Mrs. Brown begins to snore, her sixty cats have fun galore.
ISBN 0-689-83077-7
[1. Cats Fiction. 2. Stories in rhyme.] I. Oller, Erika, ill. II. Title.
PZ8.3.N4655Cat 2001
[E]—dc21
99-32226

AL BR
J
PZ8.3
.N4655
Cat
2001

Cats, Cats, Cats!

by
LESLÉA NEWMAN

illustrated by
ERIKA OLLER

Simon & Schuster Books for Young Readers

New York   London   Toronto   Sydney   Singapore

In a great big house on the edge of town
Lived a tiny old woman named Mrs. Brown

She had no children, she had no mother
She had no sister, she had no brother

She had no chickens, she had no rats
What Mrs. Brown had were . . .

cats, cats, cats!

Cats in the sunlight enjoying a snooze
While Mrs. Brown watched the eight o'clock news

Cats on the counter, each deep in a dream
While Mrs. Brown drank her coffee with cream

Cats sleeping on sofas, cats sleeping on chairs
While Mrs. Brown swept and vacuumed the stairs

Cats snoring in harmony, all in a bunch
While Mrs. Brown ate an omelette for lunch

Cats dozing outside, each one on a pillow
While Mrs. Brown trimmed the old weeping willow

Black cats, white cats, gray cats, too
Eyes of brown and eyes of blue

Eyes of gold and eyes of green
Tall cats, short cats, fat and lean

Striped cats, spotted cats, large and small
Mrs. Brown just loved them all

She loved the softness of their fur

She loved the loudness of their purr

She loved to comb their fluffy tails

She loved to manicure their nails

She loved to sit and chat with them

She loved to wear a hat with them

She loved to fill her lap with them

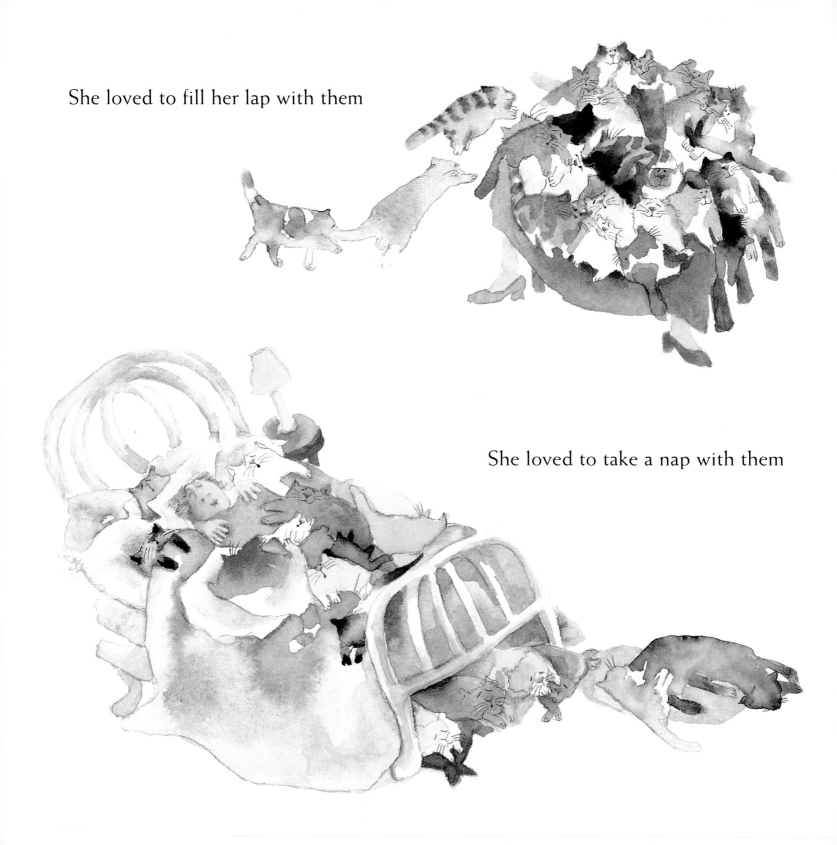

She loved to take a nap with them

She loved to place them all just so
And then embrace them row by row

When nighttime came, old Mrs. Brown
Put sixty bowls of cat food down

Then pet each cat upon the head
And marched herself straight up to bed

As soon as she began to snore
The fun began with cats galore

Cats in the entryway throwing confetti
Cats in the dining room eating spaghetti

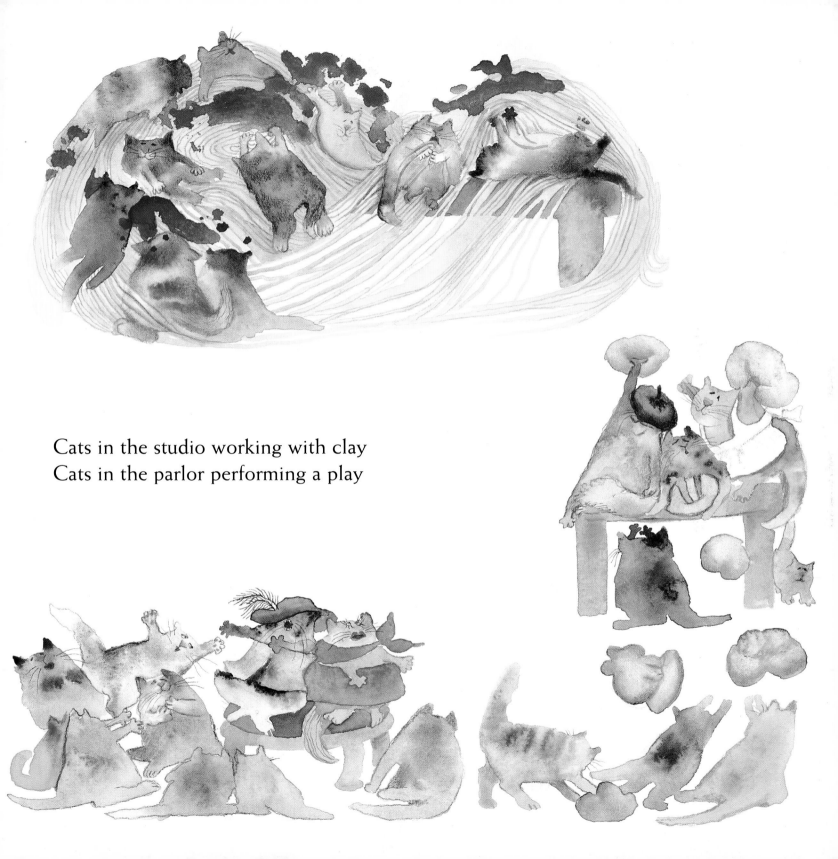

Cats in the studio working with clay
Cats in the parlor performing a play

Cats in the drawing room, purling and knitting
Cats in the sewing room having a fitting

Cats in the closet in jackets and hats
Cats in the courtyard with baseballs and bats

Cats in the library, writing and reading
Cats in the kitchen, stirring and kneading

While Mrs. Brown was tucked in tight
The cats would party every night

They'd chase their tails, they'd cut a rug
They'd fox-trot and they'd jitterbug

They'd feast on seven-layer cakes
And drink one hundred chocolate shakes

They'd whoop it up until the dawn
Those cats could really carry on

The sun came up, the cats went down
And out of bed crept Mrs. Brown

She clasped her hands up to her chest
And cried, "My cats are just the best!"

Then piled them all into a heap
So they could get their beauty sleep

Some say that Mrs. Brown is batty
And that her house is way too catty

Says Mrs. Brown, "Oh fiddle dee dee!
I love my cats and they love me."

BOOK OF
STRAYS

PHOTOS

COSMETIC
CAT CARE

NO BATHS
PLEASE

HOW CATS
SLEEP

BOSTON PUBLIC LIBRARY

3 9999 04179 336 3

Allston Branch Library
300 N. Harvard Street
Allston, MA 02134